Field Trip

More Super ♡ Duper ♡ Royal ♡ Deluxe books!

Missy's
Super ♡ Duper ♡ Royal ♡ Deluxe

Field Trip

By
Susan Nees

BRANCHES™

SCHOLASTIC INC.

For Samuel and Benjamin

Library of Congress Cataloging-in-Publication Data

Nees, Susan, author.
Field trip / by Susan Nees.
pages cm. — (Missy's super duper royal deluxe ; 4) (Branches)
Summary: On a school field trip to the state Capitol, Missy is
dissapointed to learn that there is no gift shop and decides,
along with her friend Oscar, to visit the governor to petition one.
ISBN 0-545-43854-3 (pbk. : alk. paper) — ISBN 0-545-49612-8 (hardcover: alk paper) —
ISBN 0-545-57704-7 (ebook) 1. School field trips—Juvenile fiction. 2. Gift shops—
Juvenile fiction. [1. School field trips—Fiction. 2. Gift shops—Fiction.] I. Title. II. Series:
Nees, Susan. Missy's super duper royal deluxe ; 4. III. Series: Branches (Scholastic Inc.)
PZ7.N384Fi 2014
[E]—dc23

2013027607

ISBN 978-0-545-49612-4 (hardcover) / ISBN 978-0-545-43854-4 (paperback)

12 11 10 9 8 7 6 5 4 3 2 1   13 14 15 16 17 18 19/0

Printed in China   38
First Scholastic printing, December 2013

Book design by Marissa Asuncion

Table of Contents

Chapter One
Happy Dance

This is Melissa Abigail Rose.

But everyone calls her "Missy."

This is Missy's cat Pink.

Everyone calls him "Pink."

When Missy woke up this morning, she did her happy dance.

Hip hip hooray!

I can't wait!

Today is the field trip!

It is going to be super duper fun!

Missy's class was going on a field trip to the state capitol. A field trip meant a bus ride and special snacks and no schoolwork.

And most exciting of all, a field trip
meant a gift shop!

snow globe

stickers

glitter pens

6

charm bracelet

glasses

super duper
hat

pinwheel

Once Missy got to school, she lined up by the bus. The class had to wait for their teacher, Miss Snodgrass, to call out partners for the day.

Miss Snodgrass called out the partners, two by two.

Paulette and Dexter.

Tiffany and Taylor.

Josey and Lily.

Missy and Oscar were partners. Oscar was not a talker. Oscar was a thinker.

Then Miss Snodgrass went over the trip rules. There were A LOT of rules.

Miss Snodgrass was finally finished. It was time to get on the bus.

Chapter Two
Row, Row, Row Your Boat

Missy sat next to Oscar. Oscar sat next to the window.

Oscar told Missy all about the governor. . . .

Missy had heard enough about the governor. She wiggled in her seat. She looked around the bus.

Miss Snodgrass had said it would be a long bus ride. Missy didn't mind. There was lots to do.

Lily brought crackers—just in case she got carsick.

Dexter did magic tricks.

Taylor made something out of string.

Henry taught everyone a card game called crazy eights.

Nina and Nona showed off their matching socks.

And Samuel told about the time he ate seven hot dogs.

Yup, seven hot dogs!

As the bus rumbled on, the miles flew by.

When the bus screeched to a halt, the singing stopped. There was the state capitol. It was big—super duper BIG!

The students couldn't wait to get off the bus—especially Missy.

Before going inside, Miss Snodgrass reminded the students about the most important rule of the day.

Chapter Three
The Tour

Welcome to the capitol. My name is Miss Bertha.

Inside the capitol, the tour guide greeted Miss Snodgrass and her class.

Missy looked at Oscar. Then Oscar told Missy, "A rotunda is a round room."

The students saw lots of things on the tour . . .

a flag as big as a house,

a display of the state's birds,

a lot of old pots and arrowheads,

and a room full of old maps.

The students learned about the governor.

> The governor's job is very important.

> The governor takes care of the state's money.

Missy began to wiggle and shuffle her feet. She had heard enough. She was ready for the gift shop.

Miss Bertha asked if anyone else wanted to guess. Missy smiled. She knew what the most important part of the tour was.

THE GIFT SHOP!

We always go to the gift shop before we get on the bus!

The gift shop?

No. There is no gift shop in the capitol.

After that, the tour just wasn't the same for Missy. But Miss Bertha kept talking.

All this talk about the governor and about laws gave Missy an idea.

We ARE going to meet the governor.

Yoo-hoo! Miss Snodgrass!

Chapter Four

Partners

Missy had a plan. Her plan did not include going to the bathroom.

Missy and Oscar looked for the governor's office. They found . . .

an old elevator,

a broom closet,

a man named Shorty,

and a conference room.

Missy sped down the hall. She was just about to open the door to the governor's office when Oscar stopped her.

Waaait a minute! Why do <u>you</u> want to see the governor? Does this have to do with glitter pens and snow globes?

Oscar, you are a real thinker!

The governor makes laws, right? And what this capital really needs is a gift shop, right? So, the governor can make a law that says there <u>must</u> be a gift shop here, RIGHT?!

Chapter Five

Make It Happen

Missy and Oscar walked up to the front desk.

A door opened, and a man looked out. It was the governor.

Missy and Oscar took a seat in the governor's office.

Now, what can I do for you two?

Missy got right to the point.

Well, Mr. Governor, sir, it's like this. You have a problem. A super duper BIG problem!

Mr. Governor, think about all the cool governor stuff you could have in a gift shop! Like . . . Um . . .

Just then, Oscar jumped up.

T-shirts that say "Make it happen, and make it snappy" and decoder rings and flashlights and state maps!

Missy looked the governor in the eye.

The governor sat straight up in his chair.

His face lit up.

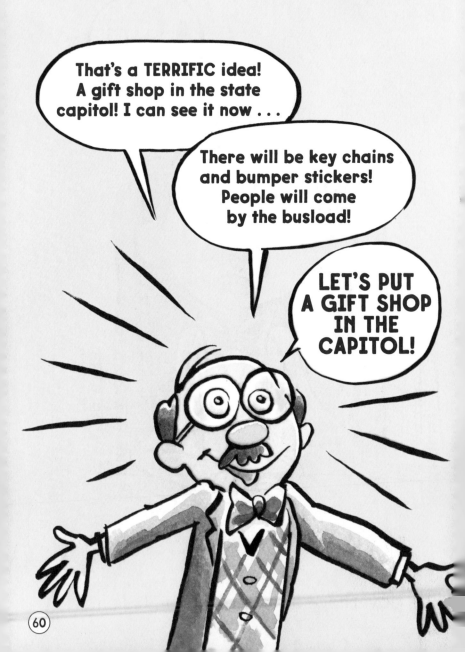

That's a TERRIFIC idea!
A gift shop in the state
capitol! I can see it now . . .

There will be key chains
and bumper stickers!
People will come
by the busload!

LET'S PUT
A GIFT SHOP
IN THE
CAPITOL!

When Missy and Oscar got up to leave, the governor gave Oscar a handshake and a campaign button that lit up.

The governor gave Missy a snow globe that played "The Star-Spangled Banner."

We need more people like you two at the state capitol.

Chapter Six
Make It Snappy

As soon as the governor heard that Missy and Oscar needed to find their bus, he made things happen.

The governor led Missy and Oscar out of the capitol and down the steps. They marched across the street.

Once they got to the parking lot, it wasn't long before they found Miss Snodgrass and the rest of their class.

Everyone cheered!

And the bus driver
honked the horn.

On the long bus ride home, Missy turned to Oscar.

Missy looked out the window.
One day she wanted to be a governor.
She would work in the capitol, and it
would have the best gift shop ever.
And her motto would be:

Make it happen,
make it snappy,
and make it—

Super Duper
Royal Deluxe!

The End

Susan Nees

went to a small school that did not take field trips. But if Susan had been able to go on a field trip, she would have been the first one on the bus and the last one out of the gift shop! Susan toured her state capitol while writing this book. Just like Missy, she wandered away from the tour. She found a janitor's closet, a grandfather clock that chimes, and a display with a two-headed snake. Missy's Super Duper Royal Deluxe is Susan's first children's book series.

MiSSY'S
Super Duper Royal Deluxe

Can you answer these questions about Field Trip?

Oscar and I have different ideas about what the field trip is about. What do we each think?

Look at page 37. What do you think the light bulb means?

Why was Missy wiggling and shuffling her feet during the tour?

What is Missy's super duper plan that she shares with the governor?

What questions would you like to ask the governor? Write a letter to your governor using **who, what, where, when,** and **how**. Draw pictures, too.

www.scholastic.com/branches